EPIC POE

THE SECRETS OF THE SACRED ARMS

HEINRICH DITTRICH is a South-African writer, composer, and artist. Born in 1993, Vereeniging, his childhood was spent in Vanderbijlpark, Gauteng, until his family moved to Secunda, Mpumalanga, where he started the first grade and spent the rest of his childhood. After High school he proceeded to study languages (including, English, French, German, Latin, and Spanish) at the North-West University in Potchefstroom, North West. This opened an opportunity for him to work in France as an English Language Assistant Teacher. After traveling back and forth between the two countries, he started teaching languages at High School. He is now pursuing the arts while working as a part-time teacher.

By Heinrich Dittrich

PROSE FICTION

A Candle Under the Water (2021)

POETRY

Hortus:
The Goldprint of the Arche (2023)
The Secrets of the Sacred Arms (2023)

CRITICISM

Towards Identifying a New Literary Genre: Stature—the Status (2021)
Perfeksioneer Afrikaans as Addisionele Taal (2023)

THE HORTUS

La Chanson des Mille Rêves

PRESENTED FROM THE

Prime Anamnesis

PART TWO

The Secrets of the Sacred Arms

HEINRICH DITTRICH

HEINRICH DITTRICH

The Secrets of the Sacred Arms

La Chanson des Mille Rêves

Symbolical Script

[INDEPENDENTLY PUBLISHED]

THE SECRETS OF THE SACRED ARMS

First published in 2023

FIRST EDITION: NOVEMBER 2023

Draft2Digital

Imprint: Independently published

Self-published

INTRODUCTION.

The Secrets of the Sacred Arms is self-published in November 2023, nine months after its prequel, *The Goldprint of the Arche.*

Although I originally planned for it to be released much earlier, I did not go on with this sequel, for I first wished to complete another language textbook. I desired to do this to grow my language knowledge with the triumphant hope that it would make me a better writer and teacher.

Not only did I indulge myself in this work, but I also revised the first edition of *The Goldprint of the Arche* soon afterwards. I have done this to rectify any contextual and conventional inconsistencies, which ultimately brings the poem's scope more in line with what I genuinely want the entirety of the epic to represent. Interested readers of the epic can find the changes made to the second edition of *The Goldprint of the Arche* in this volume under "Textual and Revisional Notes". Furthermore, the manuscript remains unedited by any other parties apart from myself.

About the manuscript

I completed the original version of the epic poem between 2017 - 2023, although I had produced some notes concerning its scope before then, as the idea had come to me before that time.

However, the poem's core only surfaced while I was working as an English Language Assistant Teacher in Strasbourg, France, around 2019. I was still unaware of what the whole thereof would turn out to be, and it would only be at the beginning of 2023 that I had finally completed the first draft of the entire poem. Nevertheless, it remains incomplete.

The reasons for this preliminary script are both conventional and contextual. Although publishing the second part of the Hortus, *The Secrets of the Sacred Arms*, brings the whole of the text closer to meeting its desired end, four-sixths of the poem remains. For, though only half of the first draft rhymes, the other part lays in free verse, while four-sixths have no accurate metre. Likewise, the scope of the poem needs a few minor adjustments.

Towards its finality, I completed it in what was a challenging time of my life. For this reason, I hope that if anybody who has ever struggled in their life would come to give their time and attention to indulge herein, it might stand as a beacon of enlightenment. And if not. Then, at least have an enjoyable story to read in epic verse.

Inspirations and motivations

It was - and still is - a work in progress; this tale that grew in my imagination until it became what it is this day. There are as many things as there aren't to coerce a person into a strenuous task, such as writing a story.

And, of all the things I can mention that have inspired and motivated me to achieve this dream, there is but one thing essential to note regarding this text—the incompleteness of ancient calligraphy. It is then that same fragmented history that holds many enigmas.

From religious texts and mythologies, legends and fairytales, conspiracies to sacred geometry, the unspoken truth remains. And from its comparison, I could draw a parallel between those times and our lives and mine. There are many things we need help understanding. Many answers we need to find. And though I wouldn't call myself an expert in these affairs, it is my curiosity that greatly inspired me and motivated me to discover some truth through fiction.

The scope of the poem

Standing in my father's garden, stargazing, I had vivid fantasies replaying time over and again in my mind until the pieces of the puzzle finally came together in a cohesive whole that made sense—the epic tale of the decay of Mars into the red planet and the formation of Earth, and all the ancient history that preceded these events.

The Secrets of the Sacred Arms thus discloses the legends of the descendants of this ancient history. In essence, it is its mysteries that initially gave rise to the origins of Mars's fall.

Arrangements and Prosody

From its minor components to its entirety, I've built the *Hortus* like a puzzle out of the Fibonacci sequence of numbers.

The manuscript thus halves itself into two primary sections, where each section further splits into three parts. Finally, each part divides itself into five scrolls or books, each consisting of eight poems.

Thus, *The Secrets of the Sacred Arms* is the second part consisting of five ancient scrolls presented amid the Prime Anamnesis in the Hortus.

Moreover, I wrote the epic poem primarily in heroic couplets.

*

But without further ado… There awaits you other surprises in the poem.

HEINRICH DITTRICH, 2023
INTRODUCTION TO THIS EDITION OF
THE SECRETS OF THE SACRED ARMS

CONTENTS.

VIII. THE SECOND SCROLL OF DESCENDANTS

IX. THE THIRD SCROLL OF DESCENDANTS

X. ICHOR

By what's gone, shall we ask to find beauty again?

PREFACE.

THE key lies within the concealed truth...

Legendary, mysterious, epical, *The Secrets of the Sacred Arms* reveals the origins that gave rise to the decay of Mars into the red planet. There are many myths, legends and ancient history surrounding this phenomenon. And though the ending is disclosed, it does not reveal all there is to be known. For so are secrets concealed. The histories are made discreet. And the truth ultimately goes forgotten in time.

The Secrets of the Sacred Arms gives the legends of the descendants encompassing Mars's fall.

The Secrets of the Sacred Arms

SCROLL VI

The Code of Chivalry Among
KINGS & KNIGHTS

THUS,
THE SCROLL MARKED KINGS AND KNIGHTS

[ARGUMENT]
The scroll of kings and knights follows Rose's appointment of a ruler of the lands of Mars after the disruption of men. Where it was once believed the embryophyte could live without such ruler, the times have proved otherwise. Moreover, it also includes the establishment of the seven kingdoms of the lands of Mars.

41. The Silence of Hortus

NOW, Hortus in their promise came complete,
The time had come the trinity to meet,
For they were now as them to there give reign,
For them to see what all become and gain.
995 Yet they were present in and out of all,
So winds and waves made him a better whole.
For whilst there had remained but two above,
But one came down to Mars to serve their love:
And though unseen and too untouched he was,

1000 He was too felt in e'ery feeling's cause;
To hope to be the ever so fixed bark,
To guide of these who wanted his embark:
For surely those who came to know them well,
They would so grant them passage in their shell.
1005 And thus, by this have times yet changed again,
Within this aeon of descendant men
The second age that thus were born to thrive,
The age of legends came to thus derive.

42. The Disruption of Men

FROM his imprisoned realm he made his mark,
O, Sedges in the shade of the cool dark.
For yet detained he had his wicked way:
Inside those minds that's weak and frail he lay.
Thus, whispers wooing in the back of mind,
So Sedges had his third form redefined.
1015 And so, distilling in those pure of hearts,
In much of those creations, evil arts.
And though they were not yet the most severe,
Those seeds would grow into a bigger fear.
As most had come to suffer under this—
1020 Their virtues turned into indifferences:
As mercies on poor souls in need weren't kept,
So, selfishness had charity o'er stepped.

43. The Foundling, the Stag, and the Secret Garden

SO Rose had seen her brother's wicked schemes,
the love she once had felt had lost its theme.
1025 And thus, the time for knights and kings become,
and so had Rose revealed herself to some.
Transformed she was a frail and helpless fawn,
And village onto village she had gone.
And so she did for a pure heart's desire
1030 (For all the Mars unknowingly require).
To only some she showed her presence dear,
As most neglect her beauty, essence clear.
Yet none had come to care much for this view,
But one stray foundling, he, who was e'er true.
1035 That day she came to show of him the course,
A boy so famished—full of great remorse.
He was no beauty as of yet, said some,
But handsome and so great he shall become.
And none in those poor villages he found
1040 To give to him some bread to go around.
(Yet there he had but one good friend he saw;
A love in him she bore against the law.)
And so he turned to the vast wood to cry,
And saw there on a hill his good reply.
1045 At first his thought proved like his current foes,
A bow and arrow he thus made to pose.
Wherein the woods he made a haunting hunt,
But by the fawn's pure gaze he was confront'd:
A stare intense upon his fairest soul
1050 That did not let him take the beast as goal.
The boy, succumbed with tears from his just eyes,
Had met the fawn on his right side as prize.

Enchanted, this fair sight had rendered them,
A seed to grow into a lasting stem.
1055 From soul-to-soul to his bare feet he ran,
And so he traced the fawn without a plan.
Thus deep into the forest's depths he went
Without concern he followed the event.
Until surprised—a sight had him revealed:
1060 The fawn had gone but so had she unsealed.
A secret garden suddenly unveiled,
Secluded from all, thus there it prevailed.
And there in the fair garth the fawn recurred
And morphed into the stag of white—matured.
1065 And there she moved along a waterfall,
And seemed as the allotter of them all.
He tailed in her mysterious of way,
Her antlers rippling in the pool's blue bay.
It yielded for a fish to swim there by,
1070 Whose tear released the future to comply:
The boy who's he, and he who held a sword.
Had joined the lands of Mars with great accord.

44. The Boy and His Sword

THE stag had relocated her abode,
her purpose clear for what's to be bestowed.
1075 So on a farther end of the garth's plants,
The stag had shown the boy the royal grants:
For there to him was shown a pearl of gold,
And as a seed it was alike, behold.
By it, of him, was asked his greatest care,
1080 For so it will remove all his despair.

For eight recurring cycles he must do,
And if one's lost all will become e'er blue.
And thus, the boy, he went and made his turns,
For eight recurring cycles he returns.
085 And on the eighth the pearl had thus transformed,
And into a fair flower it had formed.
For what a man shall find his strength in this:
A simple blooming bud without a bliss;
To look, thus, past the weak and frail, and see
090 This fragile flower—and all it can be.
The flower blossomed from a shining stone
That had concealed its mysteries unknown.
The stag that saw the power in the boy
T' unlock these secrets and them thus employ.
095 Behold! The boy, without a witness picked
The blossom from the rock without conflict.
The petals of the flower blew away,
And so the stem it made a new display:
A sword—much mightier and powerful
100 That none could ever come to overrule.
And of its name that it shall e'er record:
Carnation—and it shall serve but one lord.
Behold! The day the one true king was made
Without a penny or a costly trade.
1105 For so of virtues, he was chosen from,
And so, a man of him had too become.

45. The King, the Queen, his Knights, and Echinacea

THE boy returned as king of the most high,
Yet to convince of the new law's imply.
Though many had not trust in this new right,
1110 But eight prestigious of embryophyte,
Whose loyalty had rose to great extent,
And thus progressed to serve his represent.

"Long life our chosen king of high," they said,

And everyone soon followed the new head.
1115 And to those eight who first stepped from the crowd,
The knightly code of chivalry they vowed.
And of the maiden who had loved him dear,
The bond of unison became sincere.
And Helianthus was the name he bore,
1120 So Jasmine was the graceful queen the more.
And their he firmly stood as mercy dear,
Where grace and of divinity was clear.
And thus together congregated they
To form a fortress great and strong to stay.
1125 Echinacea was the true kingdom's name,
Where all had come to lay in its acclaim.

46. The Segregations of Powers

AND so within these epical events
There had still lain, thus, more concrete

contents.
The king had thus decid'd of a fair fate
1130 To keep the peace there in-and-out of state:
The power of the sword he will divide
In seven other swords to rule beside.
Thus to his knights crowned kingly to be more
Were given swords of power to adore:
1135 Thus: Tulip, Iris, Dahlia there came,
With Cypress and of Crocus all the same,
Gazania, Gardenia as well,
And these were thus their names that of them tell.

And thus of them were asked: "Explore the lands!
1140 To build you kingdoms and your great expands.
But of Echinacea you must hold on,
Or else the powers of the swords be gone."

47. The Establishment of the Seven New Kingdoms

THE knights who thus became of greatest kings
Went out and did as they were told of things.
1145 And there they found the seven lands of new,
With each that owned a part of a pure view.
Thus one: a hidden kingdom carved from stone,
And in the depth of desserts stood its throne.
The palace of Linaria, queens gained,
1150 So Lilac and thus Lavender there reigned.
And neither wanted too to hold the sword,
Thus Lilac's brother had become its lord.
And he was called Price Aster of good faith,

For surely, he could cleanse a soul as bathe.
1155 And they had stood for great fidelity,
Of trust and well established loyalty.
Thus two: a kingdom in the dessert sands,
Beside a flowing river it commands.
Few triangular faces there made mark,
1160 Of other features there too thus embark.
And Statice it was called; Dianthus, king,
And Alstroemeria the queen, like spring.
And thus for valour there they came to stand.
Great courage and of boldness they command.
1165 Thus three: Poinsettia on a fair shore,
A kingdom with a terminal of ore.
For there a great colossus stood of high,
As even far adrift it's seen nearby.
Hibiscus and Violet had worn the crowns,
1170 Whose presence had ne'er elected frowns.
Their righteousness was fairly there bestowed,
There in-and-out their piece and justice flowed.
Thus four, Bouvardia of blooming plants;
And there were build tall towers for their grants.
1175 Their royals were as fair as their land's grace,
Thus, Alyssum, the king all came t' embrace,
And Amaryllis was the named fair queen,
So Princess Ixia who bore their gene.
They were of honour: so respect they earned,
1180 And great esteem and boundaries them concerned.
Thus five: The palace on a mountain range,
Whose enemies could ne'er come to derange.
There, Clematis ruled over all the plains,
The queen, Lunaria, who also reigns.
1185 Anthurium this kingdom great was called,
Who brought to Mars nobility it hauled.

Thus six: A kingdom built in forests vast,
Whose temples rose in steps that all surpassed.
And Gerberas this colony was called;
1190 Who gazed upon it was fore'er enthralled.
And Ilex was the kings of strong command,
Their fortitude had come to firmly stand.
Thus seven had Bergenia displayed,
Whose greatest wonder was from marble made:
1195 With columns that around its temple raised,
Who gazed upon this style was e'er amazed.
Iberis and thus Laurel wore the crowns,
And rightly reigned there over glory's grounds.
The last of knights had no expand to built,
1200 Nor had received a sword of po'er to hilt.
Yet there in fair Echinacea he stood
To aid and so advice the high king good.
And liberty he cared for dear and well,
In secret hoping it shall once excel.
1205 And he had come to have some children too:
And Lupin and so Daisy—they were two.

48. A Time of Divinity

AT last the ends had come from these events
The whole of Rose's world thus so presents.
And thus begun the most divine of time
1210 Without more such a terrible of crime.
And thus the king and queen they had new life:
A child who Jasmine bore after the strife.
And he will come to bring content to all,
A seed of life born always to install.

SCROLL VII

The continuations of the

I DESCENDANTS

THUS

The Scroll of Descendants, the First, Marked

ACRES

[ARGUMENT]

The legends of the descendants continue: The first scroll of descendants, a.k.a. Acres, tells the legends of the embryophyte after the establishment of the seven kingdoms. It follows the corruption among men and towards the establishment of the new order on the lands of Mars. It concludes with the disclosure of the unknown creation.

49. The Corruptions among Men

OF the pure hearts of men were the most frail,
They shall so be the first to fall and fail.
So Sedges in his hidden form had gazed
upon the lands and saw content times raised.
And thus, he plott'd once more his wicked schemes
220 T' instil in men again his evil themes:
The vices and the sinful ways of life.

So in these times he shall thus cause much strife:
To teach them how to find a fast delight,
That's heated in the worlds well thrills of spite.
1225 For in his angered envy to thus rule
To come and break the spirits to be cruel.
And kill a happy smile and lose all hope,
Thus for his ends to meet his wanted scope.

50. Pea's Diabolical Dream

HIS plan was simple to bring his smear smite,
O, Sedges, in the dawn of the dark night.
His whispers woke thus Pea from a poor dream,
His whispers calling to bring his regime.
For Sedges knew the elements' close points,
He was imprisoned there within their joints.
1235 And though of one that were so close at hand,
It was protected by a sword's expand.
Yet, there was one, another not far gone,
And to its setting Pea was strangely drawn.
Thus in the night did Pea so mount his horse,
1240 And followed those duff whispers on the course
Onto a field that lead him to dismount.
And on the floor, he laid his ear t' account.
And there the whispers came from the same deep,
For all the precious stone that it must keep.
1245 And so had Pea thus rode his horse aback
For this dear deed instilled for an attack.
Thus by the rise of day he'd turned the king
To mine for gold for better riches bring.
And though the king had his own doubts to give,

1250 But Pea was confident to thus deceive.
And so the miners placed had found the gold,
And Pea his secret treasure to behold.
It was a crystal sphere as red the pearl,
And onto men it shall bring much twirl.
1255 So Sedges had not whispered any more
And spoke to Pea through this glass ball – a door.
He swore to him more power and much land,
Yet he must come t' obey of his rough hand.
And Pea agreed to all of his demands;
1260 His heart thus bitter with his new commands.

51. Queen Jasmine's Entreat

THUS Pea had called for e'ery king and queen
To join them all in court for a great scene
But curious and cautious Jasmine felt
For by a maiden, she was warned of welt.
1265 So on the night the council came to meet
Had Jasmine begged her husband to retreat:

"The walls have ears and whisper vilest things,
I fear the worst might come, and thus it brings.
I have no proof of what I speak or heard
1270 But of a servant witness and their word.
O! You, the one I love and have betrothed,
Before you were the king, I had you swathed,
And now, alas, I might not do again,
Nor you your son in this defended den!"

1275 So Jasmine tried deter her husband's way,

An ill intreat, she wants to thus delay.
As for the king, so he remained convinced,
And lift his wife for comfort he evinced:

"O! You, my wife the one of grace, I love,
1280 I trust in you, of all I place above.
But yet we should not fear but illustrate
Of e'ery virtue we accumulate.
To show our valour and thus not retire,
Stay righteous for just verdicts to inspire.
1285 To honour them as honour us decree
And noble, thus, as we all oversee.
Our fortitude shall show of po'er and strength.
So shall our glory carry us great length.
So is the pledge of liberty define,
1290 And thus we do, to do as the divine."

Before the queen could give her own reply
Arrived there, unannounced, some to comply.
So, Lilac, Lavender, and Aster came,
Of all the things to him they shall proclaim.

1295 "You speak the truth," had Lavender thus said,
"O! King, but I'd believe your wife instead."

To thus the king replied without abhor:
"What is the means of this, of your implore?"

"O! Mutiny in court, of your fair law,"
1300 So Lavender begun, "Yet we're in y' awe.
They want your head, and by the fall of night
Shall this have come to pass by coward's rite.
O! Tell me king, what is a virtue worth,

If there's not e'en an heir for its' rebirth.
1305 For if you stay, then shall it be the wait,
And if you stay, so shall it be the fate
Of the fair prince, your son, and of your wife.
Bids! The chosen line of blood of life."

In reverence the king had glanced from his
1310 Fair chamber's window for a sight of bliss:
The stag there stood with hopes and of accord:
The king was turned, and he shall be restored.

"If what you speak about is all the truth,
Yet shall I stay and thus preserve the youth,"
1315 The king replied and thus he had disclosed,
"I shall attend this summit all composed,
With Aster by my side to show the front,
The rest of you shall thus await the shunt.
For if we cannot sway the court to stay,
1320 Alas! You must thus take the prince away!"

52. Mutiny in the Court of Echinacea

AND so, the queens thus went on their own way,
As Jasmine sung the prince a song to pray.
And thus, the hour, the dureless night, drew near,
The king arrived in court without a fear.
1325 So as the doors swung open to reveal
Of him and Aster for the great appeal.
And populous it stood in silent wait,
For what it shall become—this great state.
And Aster went to stand with all the court.

1330 The king, he made his way without support.
His throne there stood so empty and so vast.
As Pea there stood around for his aghast.
A pedestal and artifact erode
And covered with black velvet, to be showed.
1335 A bid from Pea so echoed in the halls,
The king moved silently avoiding brawls.
Two guards had come before his brave advance,
But of a single word had brok'n their stance.
And 'for he could ascend his throne on high,
1340 Had Pea so intervened in vain apply.
Where in the court the matter was proposed:
A novel king of lands to be disclosed.
The claim so small and simple for decay:
Who e'er had deemed this king the royal stay?
1345 And one might so believe the convert hard.
But evil was by now in all regard.
For Pea had now proposed his right to rule,
The king appealed his claims for the fair stool.
Thus, to convince the court, Pea showed the pearl,
1350 A sight that rendered most there to unfurl.
But the keen king and Aster knew this plot.

"Alas! This's madness!" said the king his lot.

Then came to yield the power of his sword.
But lo 'nd behold the po'ers in e'en reward:
1355 For he had struck the pearl with all his might,
To break what e'er dark magic there recite.
The sight that made the great debate thus bind
The king had glanced once more the woods to find.
Behold! There from the wood it did emerge:
1360 The stag there stood for news of the converge.

"What can I do to thus appease of this?"
The king had asked the matter be dismiss.

"O, bow! Old king." had Pea thus so replied,
"Your rule is over and is hence applied."

365 But so the king refused to do this deed,
And Pea thus pulled his sword to strike for greed.
The king then signalled Aster to be set,
As Aster pulled his own to tame the threat.
Pea struck from overhead to kill the king.
370 The king had pulled his own to block the swing.
The swords thus met with thunder and of light,
Superior the sword, Carnation, fight.
The power of his sword that bound of gale
Made Pea thus hurl away to no avail.
375 Where this distraction was what they desired.
The king and Aster had their flee acquired.

53. Salvation from the Hidden Worlds

THE night was cold and full of hasty breaths,
The king thus trying to avoid all deaths.
And as he took his sword, their babe and wife,
380 He needed to preserve their bloodline's life.
And so they moved unseen through palace halls,
T' avoid of those who want to see the brawls.
And Lavender and Lilac gave the care,
Where they 'll fast met outside the palace square.
385 Two horses brought with them as tasked,

Two horses mounted—the fair future asked.
Thus Aster was there to observe the deed ,
He swore protection of the crowns' succeed.
And from the darkness the white stag emerged
1390 For the two queens and prince to be thus merged.
And though the king had asked his wife to go,
She stayed though by the king – her vows bestowed.

54. The Deaths of King Helianthus, Knight Aster, and the Execution of Queen Jasmine

FROM lighted windows servants raised their calls,
The king and party's flight from palace walls.
1395 Thus quick the party mounted each their steed,
And into the dark forest they proceed'd.
So Lavender and Lilac with the prince,
On the white stag for they the light evince.
And Aster on the one brave steed had rode,
1400 The king and queen the other steed's fair load.
So Pea and his abusive troop behind
Had chased and hunted as they were assigned.
The antlers of the stag abraded earth,
That split in two and thus had formed a firth.
1405 Of a small stream of loch had soon appeared
And followed fast by waves of water reared.
So the distraction was enough to halt
The mob in their pursuit of their assault.
And thus the party parted their own ways
1410 The three ahorse into the forest maze.
The queens and prince and stag another road.
Diversions soon completed the abode.

That pathed a way for them be doomed,
As Pea and his abusive troop resumed
1415 And so had come to follow those ahorse,
Into the forest maze without remorse.
And trailed, and trailed they gained and shrunk the
space
And saw the king's good plan of them debase.
So soon they stood in gardens fair and green,
1420 Aghast they were within this greatest scene.
The queen stood captured by the lustful foe,
And Aster stood all set to have a go.
Thus there the one true king had stood his ground,
The others thus prepared for his great sound:

1425 "O! You my brothers have thus been deceived,
Your ignorance for power is conceived.
What do you think achieves all of these deeds?
This powers you know not about its' needs."

A part in him had yearned to wield his sword,
1430 He knew though that would not be of accord.
He raised his voice one last of times and spoke:
"And you my friend? I've trusted your invoke!"

And thus he swung his sword into the air,
And planted it aback for his fair heir.
1435 And so this bravest deed had fatal ends,
One arrow met his heart without amends,
One arrow changed the times that's yet to come
As Jasmin's cries were a depressing hum..
And though in silence he had always moved,
1440 O! Hortus from his realm had disapproved.
And thus, he blessed the king with a seed great;

A gift, but yet for now in silence wait.
And from afar the stag and haul observed,
And turned towards all better things being served.
1445 So under stars and moon they rode to care
And reached Linaria by morning air,
Linaria was thus the hidden land,
No evil there could lay the child a hand.
So Aster was the queens escort from ru'ns,
1450 To palace walls now all without conflu'nce.
And yet she walked assertive and so high,
For she had never come belief of lies.
And Aster had betrayed the order new,
His loyalty of olden days in view.
1455 And so Pea took his sword to him belong,
A brand new barer of the sword so strong,
He was then punished by his brutal death.
And for a fortnight she had kept her breath,
Until the queen of late were too no more,
1460 But yet she came to raise her voice before.

"I put my trust in *you* and all our strife,
For only *you* may know the path of life."

And though in silence he had always moved,
O! Hortus from his realm had disapproved.
1465 And thus, he blessed the two with a seed great;
A gift, but yet for now in silence wait.

55. The Burial of the Crowns and the Establishment of the New Order

THUS he, who was to give away their frames,
Had come to fall onto his knees for shames.
The graces were thus met with mercy's grace,
1470 And from that night he'd met a covered face.

"You cry," the face had come to say to him,
"For you now know the truth of all the grim.
O! Give to me their bodies that endured,
A proper funeral them so insured."

1475 He did allow their taking to the place,
Where, O the three were met with proper grace.
Where, in Linaria a place of hope,
Where, there the place shall keep the epic scope.

And thus with olden days that old become
1480 A new ill order had thus so succumb.
Thus, by these men new orders were so made,
And ruled by Pea with Sedges in the shade.
And in this realm lived only deadly fear,
A novel line of heirs was made so clear.
1485 Alliances have shifted from their birth,
So, Diasy and so Lupin had their worth.

56. The Apprentice and the Master

FOR as all of his sisters have produced,
From those on mars, and seas and skies induced,
So he too have created his fair share,
1490 A creature yet unknown in its compare.

Yet of its origins was incomplete,
And thus, awaited it its state concrete.
And so had ordered her to give this rite
To someone who can bring about this fright.
1495 Thus in the mountains as they came to say,
A holy man abides the grand display.
For Hortus favoured him above the horde,
And thus, his actions yore provid'd award,
And favoured he himself was by extent,
1500 That even there he was so graced content,
For he too came to own an arm e'er dear,
Of sacred power in a secret cheer.
Thus, in disguise had she his visit pay,
And gave to him the boy of liege away.
1505 And told Mimosa of a fake affair,
Instruct the boy his arts divine and care.
To be a warrior of peace in times,
To stop if any coming brutefull crimes.
Mimosa, seemingly deceived, agreed,
1510 And thus, his plan almost to its succeed.

SCROLL VIII

The continuations of the

II DESCENDANTS

THUS

The Scroll of Descendants, the Second, Marked

OCEANS

[ARGUMENT]

The legends of the descendants continue: The second scroll of descendants, a.k.a. Oceans, tells the legends of the algae. It focuses primarily on the forbidden and shunned relationship between Lotus and Prince Lupin. It concludes with the declaration of a great war between the algae (from the sea) and the embryophyte (from the land) after the death of Nymphaea.

57. Sedges Reviles the Algae

CORRUPTION of those on the land endured,
Yet who abide in seas still were secured.
But Sedges with his wicked plots grew vile,
He would not have this content times of style.
1515 And for he could not enter their fair realm,
He had another scheme to overwhelm.

And thus, he called his puppet yet again,
O, Pea to do his deeds with wicked men.
And there he called upon him through the sphere
1520 To send his navy to the seas to clear,
And catch but each and e'ery fish that swim,
Until they start to sing a tiring hymn.
Yet from a water bowl Nymphaea heard
(For so her remnant of her powers stirred)
1525 Of e'ery wicked plot against her race,
So have the time thus came to like embrace.

58. The Swim of the Tides

FROM his fair youth had Lupin loved the seas,
Unlike his sister's greed for land unease.
Thus time and time again had Lupin's love
1530 Returned him to the seas where he above
Had found Nymphaea swim in her disguise
And she had seen the truth in loving eyes.

59. Lotus's Fair Fate Forged

DOWN under sea's fair golden palace lived
The algae and without a grim had thrived.
1535 And where the maidens roamed thus ever free
Some found some men to live under the sea.
Where they established thus their warm abode
The p'lace, Armeria Martima, stowed.
Yet Lotus still had roamed the oceans 'lone,

1540 Nymphaea kept her oath and he his own.
Behold! As his fair fate had thus come by
Nymphaea came disclosed to thus apply,
Of him yet one more task was thus assigned,
For all his world will soon thus come and find.
1545 And yet this vital task will bear great strife,
If so in vain, it means the end of life.
But so she had her oath of fortune set,
For she had seen the eyes to meet this threat.

60. The Fisherman's Tale

ON a fair morning Lupin was thus send
By Pea for things offshore to meet its end.
And though he was unwitting of intent,
He was impressed by simpler of consent.
For by the prince's heart was pure and soft,
The king despised this matter thus aloft.
1555 From shore the king's fair son and navy went
With a flotilla for an ill event.
With poison and their nets into the blue,
Aghast the prince their stood in his review.
His ignorance and fear made him assist
1560 With much the means in him to thus resist.
In hast the underwater guards had swum
To Lotus bearing news that left them numb.
And one more thing that was so ever worse,
The fishermen had thrived in their adverse.
1565 For some of them, alas, thus spiked were they,
As others seized in nets and moved away.
So swiftly Lotus set his novel course,

The fate he vowed and needed thus enforce.
Nymphaea told him to refrain his fork,
1570 Another will arrive to be a stork.
And there he came and there he thus had freed,
Unfortunate by some had death exceed.
And yet upon the last he had secured,
Was he thus caught by nets (his fate allured).
1575 And as they trawled him up from the seabed
Onto the deck were bare his fins he shed.

"Behold!" A fisherman had said "A fish!
Dear Prince, the king be proud you caught a dish."

Aghast the prince had stared at what he'd done,
1580 His father will be proud to call him Son.

"Now kill the fish!" he said, so worse arose,
And threw the prince a spear, "let's feed them crows!"

In disbelieve had Lupin looked at him,
He's only heard his sister's speech of grim.
1585 And as they gazed into each other's eyes,
A deeper meaning thus meant to arise.
He shied the spear and rather grabbed his sword,
And cut the knot that Lotus tied and stored.
An act that made them beat him to the ground,
1590 As Lotus's recognition was profound.
Where from the boat he jumped over the board
The fleet returned to shore without reward.

61. Oaths and Good Omen

O! Lupin was then met without a grace,
As dashing hopes that made him feel from
place.
1595 While down by under in the seas he swam,
O! Lotus with a heart and feels of damn.
And thus he took the Coral to redress,
And to Echinacea he went t' express.
And so behold of him did they thus greet,
1600 A tidal wave had first them come to meet,
And as the water pulled back down the shore,
Emerged he from the waters like before.
And as he walked, the waters had him draped,
Until he entered the ill court that gaped.
1605 And Lupin there had looked upon his grace,
And heard how Lotus came appeal the case.

"This, Pea, shall be the first and last of times
You ought to organise such bloody crimes."

"Or what!" the king replied so spitefully.

1610 Which granted him an answer rightfully,
Of solemn silence and severe decrees,
And thus pursued his leave with all unease.
And yet before his exit did take place,
His eyes and Lupin's did again embrace.

62. Forbidden Love

CAN love then be forbidden by the sight,
Forbidden only then by men's delight?
For all this time of great misfortune strive,
Had Lotus's waiting heart thus come alive.
And though what Lupin saw had left an awe,
1620 And craved to see this vision well once more.
Thus, in the sea he bathed, and bathed again,
In hopes to reconcile a love. Amen.
Behold! As thus his hopes and dreams came true,
O! Lotus came from under the deep blue,
1625 But yet as he came close as close as hearts
Did Lupin not thus seen this face of arts,
For as he Lotus did emerge did salt,
So Lupin lost his sight but felt exalt,
For as he came so close, as close as lips
1630 Can be without a kiss to thus eclipse,
Yet did he whisper in his ear a word.
And thus before his eyes and his concurred
Did Lotus swim aback into the sea,
For so if this was meant to be it be.
1635 And yet they went apart, their heart did not,
So Lupin thus returned to the fair spot.
And time and time again he did this deed,
As Lotus watched him from afar succeed.
Until they shall yet meet again unchained,
1640 And thus, together they may be ordained.
Thus he had come as close as his fair part,
And their they came as close as heart to heart.
For where their faithfulness has proved the rite
Thus were they not as star crossed as the night.

645 Thus for four seasons of their hearts and Mars's
They met each other under the bright stars.
And so they did as lovers life and dance
In secret had this grown into romance.
Until their lips had kissed and locked their fate,
650 A kiss too witnessed proud by Daisy's hate.
Their love had grown to be a willing kind,
Which neither had believed they could e'er find.
And Lupin was the first to state this sense,
As Lotus so revered with great expense.
655 So Lotus glazed upon him with sad eyes,
How could he ask his lover this in size.

"My Love. I wish I could so ask of thee
To run away and come away with me.
But yet that means to ask of you the act
660 To leave your place of birth to be exact."

To thus had Lupin then replied the fate,
And wanted not to be thus bound by weight.

"If they will come condemn of my select
It is not I, but them to leave effect."

665 So Lupin thus returned to palace walls
To tell his family of all he calls.
But yet had found that Daisy's gossip came
Before his own and thus he was to blame.
And not a single blessing nor the light
670 Was placed on him by them by all their spite.
And yet before they could have laid more harm,
Or even lock him up for the alarm,
He came to thus escape those palace walls,

Unwitting of his sisters grave appals.

63. The Death of Nymphaea

O! Daisy in the darkness she had raised,
Her father's sword had soothed and thus appraised.
Thus on a sailing ship he took ashore,
As Daisy lay in waiting to make war.
The ship had come and reached its destined mark,
1680 And Daisy him confronted from the dark.
And as she wielded thus her father's sword,
It made him jump for mercy overboard.
Where in the deep did Lotus thus arrive,
In rescuing his lover from the dive.
1685 A kiss thus under the deep blue had made,
His lover grow and thus alike displayed.
And with the power he of seas command,
By faith so took the Coral to withstand,
And send the ship to shore to be thus docked,
1690 Where Daisy wanted more for she was shocked,
So, from the ship she came to leap as well.
She'd have thus death to her or them excel.
Again by seas he made her haul ashore,
Again she made amends to the sea floor.
1695 But as she did, Nymphaea her receive,
As from the waters she arose to grieve.
Her beauty as he made her once ago
Perceived by Daisy so she may thus know.

"Thus love has come to find your brother dear

1700 A love that longs to find in you no fear.
O! Tell to me what else you crave to find
And why you feel this feel you thus declined.
Is it your fear or envy of the rule?
For so, let me then show to you the pool."

1705 And then she made her fins to thus review,
Yet Daisy had despised it and withdrew.

"I'm not a fish," did Daisy thus declare.

Nymphaea understood of the affair.
And thus she did bid well and left the shore,
1710 And turned into her form as yet before ,
And so she swam in the sea's tides away.
Enraged was Daisy thus in the dismay,
And plunged her father's sword into the sand.
That made the soil do her corrupt command,
1715 Which heated, vaporised and raised the bed,
Thus trawled the fish, a path to her had led.
And in her anger did she slit the fish,
In half it lay and thus made true her wish.
And though in silence he had always moved,
1720 O! Hortus from his realm had disapproved.
And thus, he blessed of her with a seed great;
A gift, but yet for now in silence wait.
But yet in spirit did she raise the sea,
And thus had made a wave to pay the fee.
1725 And as the water she did represent,
That crashed on Daisy for her ill intent.
And there where dreaded Daisy thus had drowned,
The king and queen had her there sadly found.
And thus to Lotus who was king no more,

1730 An higher purpose him thus now instore.
And Lupin who had thought to be a prince,
No king to be was he to thus evince.
Divine were they by now the death revealed,
O! Under water where they were concealed.

64. Declarations of Wars: Sea vs Land

AND by unfortunate events, declared
Two armies, sea and land, for war prepared.
And yet it was from all a simple source:
Deception from those vices they endorse.

SCROLL IX

The continuations of the

III DESCENDANTS

THUS

The Scroll of Descendants, the Third, Marked

ATLAS

[ARGUMENT]

The legends of the descendants continue: The second scroll of descendants, a.k.a. Atlas, tells the legends of the Ionantha. It follows the Tillandsia's attempt to save the Mars from all it's corrupted ways. Yet, it was met in vain. For in this effort, Sedges had come to infiltrate their realm as well.

65. The Succession of Schemes

O! Sedges in the shade of the cool dark,
Thus felt elated by his great embark.
Yet of his scheme still laid there incomplete,
For worse of things that will thus come and meet.
Alas! He felt his power rising back,
Yet of his lust for more had known no lack,
1745 And would not stop no matter the offend,
Two more he needed thus to meet their end.

66. Rose Returns to Grieve Her Sister's Death

THUS from that place of safety she returned,
O! Rose, as stag, had been thus so concerned,
For she had felt her sister's death and deeds,
1750 Deceptions much that to a war great leads.
And of her fate on her ill brothers hand,
To seek her blood and take over the land.
Thus had she come to thus escape the prince,
For a fair hope of chance to thus evince.
1755 Behold! As it then was a dreadful sight,
The stag there moved on shores of the sick fight.
And there she found her sister thus in two,
And shed a tear for all that were in view.
And then had Sedges in his weakness come,
1760 And whispered there his dissonant, ill hum.
And though he'd lust for shedding blood and harm,
His curse then be of him to thus disarm.

"O! Dearest Brother what then have you done,
We used to be then e'er the closest one.
1765 What have I e'er done to deserve this fate?
Because at all the cost you house much hate."

And thus he did not come to her reply,
With wellness but his vileness to apply.

"Your time, o, sister has then come e'er near,
1770 And even now then as we speak you fear.
Of all of me and all that I began,
O! Of more illness is thus in the plan.
Another I have set in this great scheme,

And more commit to do my vilest dream!"

775 And then they parted each their separate ways,
Thus, all in all awaiting the great phase.

67. Butzii's Change of Heart

WHILE all of these events were housed on Mars,
Tillandsia beheld them from the stars.
And thus, she called and send her pride below,
780 To thus account for all that weren't on show.
So Butzii flew over the changed land,
To thus record to all thus understand.
Alas! And as he did, he faced deceit,
O! Sedges him convinced of his elite.
785 There in the secret garden once bestowed,
But now a place that came to thus erode.
And there he found and heard some whispers weird,

"Who are you?" Butzii's demand thus feared.

"O! You the one of pride remembers. No!
790 As I do you. Desire you to know?
These secrets, I thus keep with me of you,
Your fairest mother knows well of it too.
Yet there you stay believing her fair lies,
Much more there waits for your imply.
795 Thus go to her, creator of the sky
Tell her to send a teacher from the high,
For of the lands of mars came to decay,

And needs a mentor's guide for a new day.
O! Then shall I reveal to you the lie,
1800 Of greater things you thus come to supply."

And in his heart had Sedges spoke his word
And from his heart had changes thus occurred.

68. Buzzii's Influence

HIS lust for po'er and knowledge grew by day,
And thus he'd do as told to get his way.
1805 He went to his creator to express,
To help restore the land their faithful bless.
And though at first, she came to hesitate,
Then he told her of Sedges and his state.
That death awaits her sister's fragile life,
1810 And if not be to thus avoid this strife.

69. Brachycaulos Descends

O! Brachycaulos she thus send to land,
His gift of mercy's well in grave demand.
Yet she had warned him of the harmed deceit,
To be aware; from what he must retreat.
1815 And thus, he did descend there from the sky
To teach the embryophyte virtues high.
Inevitable evils he thus met,
Yet so disguised and pure as any threat.
So Sedges came and spoke to Pea again,

1820 To fake his grieve for all he had back then.
For Brachycaulos will thus to him come,
And when he does of grieve he must become.
Thus soon he did thus come to Pea to speak,
To thus convince him better things to seek.

1825 So Pea had faked and thus seduced him great,
And spoke to him in grieve to thus debate.
"O! Long have I then been seduced and thralled,
Until my son and daughter death installed.
O! Evil and its power I dismiss,
1830 And may it be that I become more bliss."

"Where is this evil you so fear in doubt,
Of it we must thus rid and be devout."

"There in the forest deep it lurks and prays,
For all the wickedness him so obeys.
1835 Where all the core of evil there they start,
And if you'd kill it, troubles will depart.
And then back home you may then go return."
Had so said Pea to please his great concern.

70. The Death of Rose

SO Brachycaulos then to go assess
Had taken Pea with him to thus address.
And to the forest as they thus had gone,
Pea took the pearl, of him had made a pawn.
And as the beast saw Pea in the good space,
She had reacted with a fearful face.

1845 And by the curse the pearl had brought within,
Had Brachycaulos only seen fake skin.
The quick attack had Brachycaulos viewed,
His spear set strong for death to be endued.
And as he did so spear the beast's feared heart,
1850 The vision of a beast him thus depart.
And though in silence he had always moved,
O! Hortus from his realm had disapproved.
And thus, he blessed dear Rose with a seed great;
A gift, but yet for now in silence wait.
1855 He sought but to protect, and she the same,
Thus unaware of what they shall acclaim.
And as his gaze had met Pea's spiteful smile,
His tears met ichor from this helpless trial.

"What have I done, my hand, to shed this blood?"
1860 So Brachycaulos said and fell to mud,
"My judgements shall thus judge me for this stunt.
Forgive me mother of this condemned hunt!"

71. The Death of Brachycaulos

PEA'S faithful troops had followed them too close,
And found them all on forest grounds morose,
1865 And quick before the son from skies could flee,
They caught him by the wings to make their plea.

"You've killed our goddess," have they cried out loud,
"Of great the consequence this be endowed."

And thus, before the people of the land,
1870 They tied his wings and limbs to thus withstand.
And put him on a stage to be displayed,
And slaughtered him for all he had betrayed.
And though in silence he had always moved,
O! Hortus from his realm had disapproved.
1875 And thus, he blessed of him with a seed great;
A gift, but yet for now in silence wait.

72. Declarations of Wars: Sky vs Land

THE word had travelled fast into the skies,
And unaware of all the word belies.
But for the death of her dear son was spent,
1880 And for the death of Rose had no content,
The skies and land so vowed to each a war,
All ignorant the truth the falseness bore.

SCROLL X

The first key of secrets:

ICHOR

THUS

The Scroll Marked Ichor

[ARGUMENT]
The final scroll of *The Secrets of the Sacred Arms*, Ichor, follows Butzii's confrontation with his creator about the secrets of their past, mythological lives. It tells the end of the age of legends and concludes the prequal to what will result in the great war of Mars.

73. Butzii's Faded Destiny

SO after all the dreaded deeds were done,
Had Butzii thus set out from the son.
885 And Sedges he had found there in the sphere,
For all the things that he had set in fear.
Thus, Butzii has done as Sedges said,
And thus, revealed to him his secret stead.
A secret him had longed to touch his seal,
890 Behold! He did recall all did conseal.
And then his anger he began to taste,

For where his mother him thus so had placed.

"By blood of your creator on your hands,
Shall this fulfill of your desired demands."

74. Butzii's Enunciation

THEN Butzii had set his maker's mark,
To thus confront of all this great remark.
And there he found her on a cloudy cliff,
With all her thoughts in mind that made her stiff.
And glancing over all the land and sea,
1900 And shedding tears to all her sisters' plea.
And yet he greeted her with greed and hate,
So soon his reign shall be the great debate.

"I came here to my youthful days regard,
And here I did return without a guard.
1905 I know why you have set your course to me,
I saw it well the day you came from sea,"
She said as she thus kept her silent gaze.

"Then turn around and face my newest praise."

"I shall not look at what you have become,
1910 As you attempt to take the life, you're from."

"You kept away from us your great resolve,
In gods among these realms, we can evolve."

"And yet that is not our intent, my son,

Of all the good and love I let you won.
1915 And yet you urge a darkness over all,
Though most the beauty you thus so install.
Your wants, how ignorant they made of you,
O why? Your beauty has deceived you too?"

"You know me, you know thus my reasons why."

1920 "Of many things I know but not this lie."

75. The Death of Tillandsia

AND hence their speech of twists and turns
complete,
Had Butzii thus draw his whip to meet
Her heart there on the cliff without a cry,
And made her fall to land from the high sky.
1925 And though in silence he had always moved,
O! Hortus from his realm had disapproved.
And thus, he blessed of her with a seed great;
A gift, but yet for now in silence wait.

76. The Unforgiving Witness

THE land whereon she lay the golden shore,
An algae maiden had thus seen the score.
And saw how Butzii had tailed the fall,
And as he looked upon the end of brawl.
And though the maiden thought to be disguised,

Her presence had thus Butzii apprised.

77. Arrival of the Birds

THEN those who dwell with him in the high sky
Came down below, they heard of his false cry.
And so, he blamed the maiden in the sea,
Who thought and knew and was the watchful key.
Usneoides was the one who flew,
1940 Before the algae maiden had withdrew,
And there without a doubt in rage he killed
The poor young maiden whom the truth instilled.

78. Declaration of Wars: Sea vs Sky

AND soon the gossip reached the sea-god's ear,
And thus by lies as lies be told by fear,
1945 Declared he war against the highest sky,
For what they've done, so was his grave reply.
Thus now had come the unpredicted times,
Of all three races thought of brutal crimes
The sky against the sea against the land
1950 All by the wickedness that it had planned.

79. The End before the End

AND so the age that had much prominence,
Then failed to show of its good opulence.

And thus the age of legends met its end,
And thus gave rise to ancient times' content.

80. Ichor

THUS if by blood these secrets so conceal,
Alas! By blood the sacrifice reveal.
For blood the bond of covenants behold,
So blood then be more virtuous then gold.
If death then be the start of the design,
1960 Amen! Shall we thus be reborn divine.

CONCLUDING NOTE.

Thus, this concludes the second age of the aeon of the descendants (the age of legends) that gives rise to the ancient histories of Mars. Henceforth, this remains, and it will give much assistance to comprehend the ancient histories to come.

THE END OF
THE SECRETS OF THE SACRED ARMS

GLOSSARY OF CHARACTERS AND ARTIFACTS, AND SETTINGS.

This glossary includes all characters, artifacts and settings from both this volume of *The Secrets of the Sacred Arms* and its prequal, *The Goldprint of the Arche.*

*Note:
The pronunciation of certain character and artifact names is given. The pronunciation of these words is given merely to understand how they were implemented in the rhythm of the poem and is not intended to replace their actual pronunciation.

A

Algae, The race of A race of mermen and mermaids created by Nymphaea.

Alstroemeria The queen of Statice.

Alyssum The king of Bouvardia.

Amaryllis The queen of Bouvardia.

Andreana (/ˈæn drə ɑː nə/) One of the members of the High Ionantha created by Tillandsia.

Anthurium A kingdom build on mountains.

B

Bergenia A kingdom build on the plains of Mars that was known for its beautiful architecture, displaying many columns and temples.

Botanica Also known as the Third Realm. Created by Hortus before the shaping of the Cosmos and the three worlds.

Bouvardia A kingdom filled with hanging gardens.

Brachycaulos (/ˈbrə kɪ kɔ ləs/) One of the members of the High Ionantha created by Tillandsia.

Bulbosa (/bʌlˈboʊ zɑ/) One of the members of the High Ionantha created by Tillandsia.

Butzii (/ˈbut zɪ aɪ/) One of the members of the High Ionantha created by Tillandsia.

C

Carnation The sword created by Rose in the transferal of power.

Clematis The king of Anthurium.

Coral A golden fork given to Lotus to help him rule over the seas.

Crocus One of the seven swords of power.

Cyanea (/ˈsaɪ ə nɪ ə/) One of the members of the High Ionantha created by Tillandsia.

Cypress One of the seven swords of power.

D

Dahlia One of the seven swords of power.

Dahlia Pea's wife.

Daisy Pea's daughter.

Dianthus The king of Statice.

E

Elements of Pearl, The The fruit of the opposite tree harvested by Sedges in the cursed crusade, as well as the last fruit harvested to render the Algae and Ionantha immortality.

Embryophyte, The race of The race of men and women created by Rose.

F

Fuchsii (/ˈfyu ʃɪ aɪ/) A golden rod given to Cyanea.

Fuego (/ˈfyu goʊ/) The bow and arrows given to Usneoides.

G

Gardenia One of the seven swords of power.

Gazania One of the seven swords of power.

Gerberas A kingdom build in a forest.

Goldprint of the Arche, The (*also shortened and referred to in the poem as* the Goldprint) The print found in the Realm of Hope and used for creational purposes.

H

Helianthus The high king of Echinacea and owner of the Carnation who first came to rule the lands of Mars until he decided to transfer some of his powers over to his knights.

Hibiscus The king of Poinsettia.

Hortus The prime mover and original creator of Botanica and the Second Realm.

I

Iberis The king of Bergenia.

Ilex The king of Gerberas.

Infernal Brigade, The The rebellion against the views of Hortus.

Ionantha, The race of (/ˈaɪ oʊ nən θə/) A race of beings with wings created by Tillandsia to live in the sky and clouds.

Iris One of the seven swords of power.

J

Jasmine The queen of Echinacea and beloved wife of Helianthus.

L

Laurel The queen of Bergenia.

Lavender One of the queens of Linaria.

Lilac One of the queens of Linaria.

Linaria A hidden kingdom in a desert. The palace is also cut from stone mountains.

Lotus The first merman created by Nymphaea to rule over the sea.

Lunaria The queen of Anthurium.

Lupin Pea's son and lover of Lotus.

M

Mars The prime setting of the *Hortus*.

Maxima (/ˈmæk sə mə/) A two edged sword given to Bulbosa.

N

Nymphaea (/nɪˈfi ə/) One of the members of the Vesica Pisces. The creator of the world under water.

P

Pea The knight appointed by Helianthus to be his trusted advisor who at ends betrayed his liege.

Poinsettia A kingdom build next to the ocean.

Prince Aster Lilac's brother. Also the keeper of Tulip.

Princess Ixia Daughter of King Hibiscus.

R

Realm of Hope, The The unseen realm. Also where Sedges is imprisoned.

Rose One of the members of the Vesica Pisces. The creator of the lands of Mars.

S

Sacred arms, The A series of arms given to some beings (created by the trinity sisters) for means of protection and preservation of peace.

Second Realm, the The Cosmos, including Mars, created by the Vesica Pisces.

Sedges A member of the Vesica Pisces and the leader of the rebellion; creator of the Cosmos excluding Mars.

Stag, the Rose's morphed form after the transferal of powers. (Also the fawn.)

Statice A kingdom found in a desert next to a river.

T

Tetrad siblings, The *See* Vesica Pisces.

Tillandsia A member of the Vesica Picsces and the creator of the Ionantha.

Tree of Life, The The tree bearing the fruit of life.

Trinity sisters, The The three *sisters* forming part of the Vesica Pisces.

Tulip One of the seven swords of power.

U

Usneoides (/ʌsˈni oʊ aɪ diz/) A member of the High Ionantha, created by Tillandsia.

V

Velvet Gate, The A Velvet curtain behind which the Goldprint of the Arche is put.

Vesica Pisces, The The creators of the second realm.

Violet The queen of Poinsettia.

INDEX OF TITLES.

INDEX OF FIRST LINES.

W

TEXTUAL AND REVISIONAL NOTES.

TO avoid any ambiguities, I've here included the changes of the second edition of the Goldprint of the Arche.

*Note that the new lines are cited.

Line 51. His voice arose on th' edge before my mess,
62. Within the constellations: my 'nner Mars.
63. The sight of goodness in the middle-night,
104. By dreadful terrors of the dark—they grieved.
96. Stanza separated from line 97.
110. As all awaited desperately for hears.
153. Behold! There was the aeon of, thus, Om
154. And all the ages came from this aplomb.
177. That for the first of realms they knew to be,
182. The Goldprint of the Arche they too found:
184. As if it's the pure heart of hope in frame.
185. As compass for all time and space, it stood,
191. So therefore, in their likeness as the wind,
199. Thus Hortus, in their parts, considered fame,
207. And for this reason, Hortus made their choice:
214. The space of void to change was imminent.
217. (And thus the first of aeons came complete,
218. That pathed the way for imminent replete.
219. And so the age the first creations came

220. Within the aeon of creations' aim.)
225. And so, a chaos born by this effect.
229. And as a seed of life to pollinate,
230. Its air's intent was thus set to create.
232. Into a beautiful, bright egg of life.
245. Then Hortus spoke again with all their might,
246. A sound of wind from silence and delight.
255. And though together they were named of life,
256. Alone: of spirit and of ethos rife.
272. The tree of life there gave enlightenments.
321. Thus this had come to mark the ending of
322. The first creation's age so set above,
323. A herald thus for what became the next,
324. The second age of the creation flexed.
434. Two was the tree of life all overwhelm.
363. Thus by the dance of their four loving hands,
399. And to conceal its po'er from every sight,
489. As pearls yet each their own of shapes to be,
504. As all threw fire for what they greatly yearn.
519. Give up your fight and come with us away.
543. He broke the chains and breathed fire in th' air!
569. The dragon's form thus then from him departs,
580. Stanza separated from line 581.
582. Stanza attached to line 583.
600. For I've too seen a part of its great field.
654. He lay and glanced upon the light's display:
678. So Hortus called the sisters for increase.
728. The airlads and airdames had come to fly.
743. And as all ages need to meet their end

744. So were the second age and aeon spent.
745. And as they had thus come to their complete
746. It pathed the way for imminent replete.
756. To bring their children down to decent den.
758. They had explained to them of the new law.
759. There in Botanica they called the four,
769. Their air was now maternal warm and kind.
771. And she was dressed in a white robe of silk,
772. Her hair and skin that glittered showed her ilk.
773. She held the infants in her arms devout,
781. And from the tree she plugged them leaves to b' eased,
787. She raised them in and under the liv'ng tree,
794. And hair that veiled his ears, were white as snow.
813. Thus, there at every given night, she spoke
816. How they at first made all and all declare.
827. So look into the eye of hope and see,
873. The aeon of descendants thus commenced,
874. The age the first of gold thus had dispensed.
912. Where they 'll were kept from the ill fate to die.
917. And by the grace of Hortus who had first
918. Created them thus to destroy the cursed,
919. To them again be so disposed as once,
920. To keep the balance from the treated, dunce.
933. To Brachycaulos, Gardneri bestowed,
934. A spear to keep of mercy well a code.
961. Their powers thus were locked inside the arms
962. Yet of it only some they kept their charms.
987. Where now they lurk and waited for revenge,

SIT LAVS DEO PATRI

Milton Keynes UK
Ingram Content Group UK Ltd.
UKHW010625291123
433416UK00005B/343